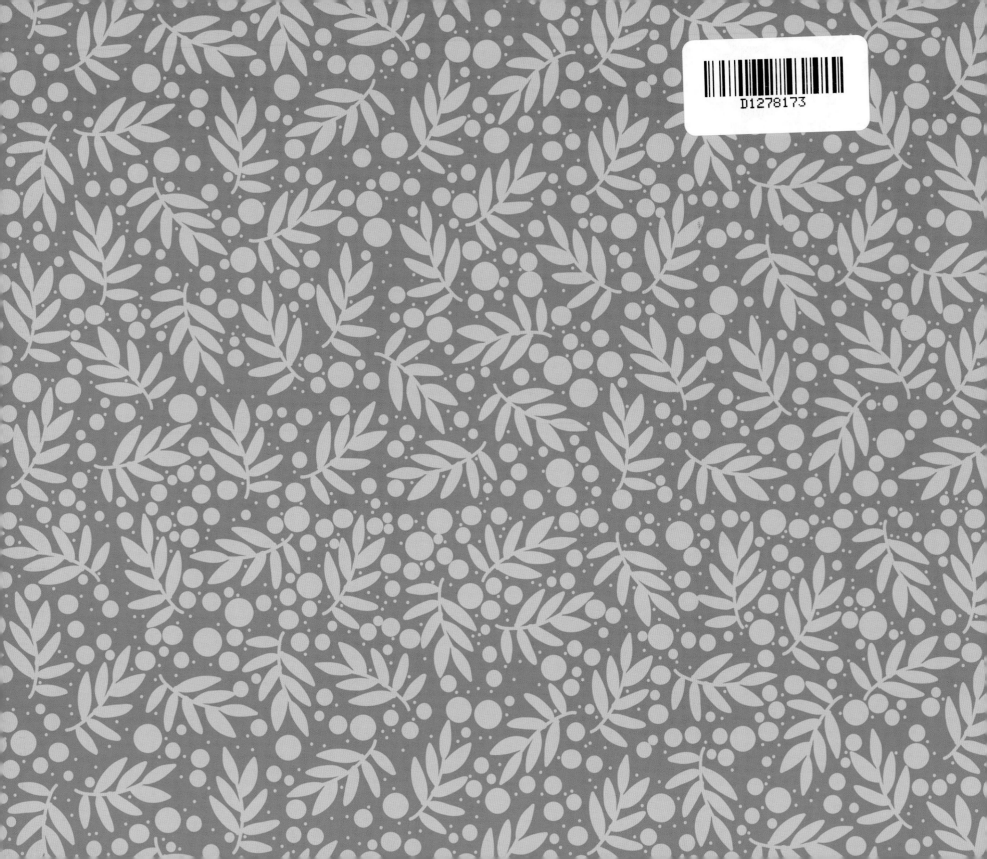

ZONDERKIDZ

Over in a Stable
Copyright © 2020 by Suzanne Nelson
Illustrations © 2020 by Aleksandar Zolotić

Requests for information should be addressed to:

Zonderkidz, 3900 Sparks Drive SE, Grand Rapids, Michigan 49546

Hardcover ISBN 978-0-310-76112-9
Ebook ISBN 978-0-310-76113-6

Editor: Barbara Herndon
Art direction and design: Ron Huizinga

Printed in China

20 21 22 23 24 / DSC / 20 19 18 17 16 15 14 13 12 11 10 9 8 7 6 5 4 3 2 1

OVER IN A STABLE

Written by Suzanne Nelson

Illustrated by Aleksandar Zolotić

ZONDERkidz

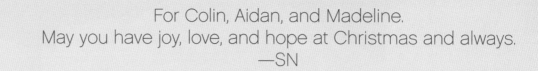

For Colin, Aidan, and Madeline.
May you have joy, love, and hope at Christmas and always.
—SN

To my children, and the brightest shine in
their eyes, to guide me eternally.
—AZ

Over in a stable, under starlight bright as sun,

stood a little drummer boy and his tattered drum one.

"Rum-pa-pum," said the boy.

"Rum-pa-pum," tapped the drum.

And they rum-pa-pummed a birthday song to welcome a wee son.

Over in a stable in a cloak of powder blue,

rested one tender mother and her loving arms two.

"Cradle," said the mother.

We cradle, rocked the two.

And they cradled a sweet bundle,

that was cuddly, soft, and new.

Over in a stable, after traveling land and sea,

came camels from afar and their noble wise men three.

"Bow," said the camels.

"We bow," said the three.

And they bowed their heads down low,

giving gifts on bended knee.

Over in a stable nestled cozy on the floor,

dozed one mother cow and her spotted calves four.

"Snuggle," said the mother.

"We snuggle," said the four.

And their snuggles warmed a manger for a prince born poor.

Over in a stable, where the miracle arrived,

stood one mother donkey and her playful donkeys five.

"Watch," said the mother.

"We watch," said the five.

And they watched in awe and wonder as God's promise came alive.

Over in a stable, in a nest of down and sticks,

sat one mother dove and her fluffy hatchlings six.

"Coo," said the mother.

"We coo," said the six.

And their coos brought dreamy smiles to the sleeping child's lips.

Over in a stable, bringing tidings down from heaven,

glowed one archangel and soaring angels seven.

"Sing," said the angel.

"We sing," said the seven.

So they sang in joyous chorus, "Unto us this child is given!"

Over in a stable, though the hour was growing late,

grazed one mother sheep and her fleecy lambs eight.

"Give," said the mother.

"We give," said the eight.

And they gave their hay to make a bed to rest a King so great.

Over in a stable, with their staffs made of pine,

marveled one loyal shepherd and his faithful shepherds nine.

"Pray," said the shepherd.

"We pray," said the nine.

And they lifted prayers of peace and grace up to the Great Divine.

Over in a stable, in a humble, holy glen,

lay one baby filling hearts of hopeful children ten.

"Love," said the baby.

"We'll love," said the ten.

And they loved the tiny baby, born the son of God and men.

Over in a stable, on a merry Christmas morn,
can you count all those who celebrate
the special babe just born?